to Maryann
because we love her

My name is Patrick Edward Parker,
and I'm not like other kids.
I don't want to be special or anything.
I just want to be like everybody else.

A kid at school called me, "Retard."
My Dad said to forget it.

How do you do that?

The problem is I'm not so smart.
The first time I KNEW I was dumb
was in first grade.
I'm not as dumb as Harold though.
He failed kindergarten.

I don't read so good
        and I'm really stupid at math.
                The truth is I can barely add.

I hate school! I JUST HATE IT!!
I never get a happy-face sticker. Hardly ever.
When they divide up teams for the spelling contest,
I get picked last except when Marvin's at school.
He's mental.

Once at recess David said,
    "How does it feel to be the
    dumbest person
    who ever lived, PAT-RICK??"

It doesn't feel good.
That's how.

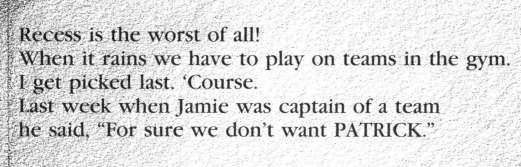

Recess is the worst of all!
When it rains we have to play on teams in the gym.
I get picked last. 'Course.
Last week when Jamie was captain of a team
he said, "For sure we don't want PATRICK."

"You take him.
No, you take him."

Then the teacher said, "Patrick, you go with Team A."
Jamie said, "Guess we're stuck with you."

Team A lost.

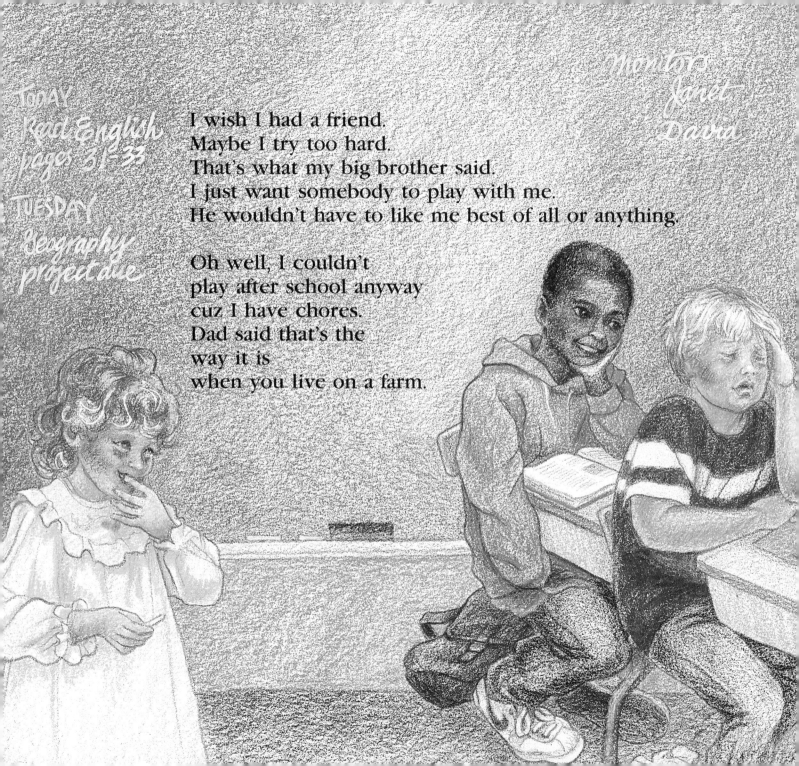

I wish I had a friend.
Maybe I try too hard.
That's what my big brother said.
I just want somebody to play with me.
He wouldn't have to like me best of all or anything.

Oh well, I couldn't
play after school anyway
cuz I have chores.
Dad said that's the
way it is
when you live on a farm.

Jamie (he's the mean one) calls me
    Patrick "Porker," instead of Parker
    or, "All beef Patty."
Once when I walked past his desk he said,
    "Hey now, THAT'S a meat ball."

Does he think
I got fat on purpose?
My name is Patrick . . .
That's my name
and I don't want
to be called anything else.

When I was waiting for the school bus one day,
Jamie said,
     "What's the matter with you?
      My Mom says your parents
      don't help you learn.
      Me, I say you're STUPID!"

Janet heard it all and made an awful face and said,
     "Duuuuuuuuuuuuh"
like I WAS stupid.

They sat in front of me on the bus and whispered in a chant,
     "Patrick is a loser . . . couldn't win if he *had* to.
     Patrick is a loser . . . couldn't win if he *had* to."

I hate it when we have to
work problems on the blackboard!
Especially math problems.
Usually I just stand there
like I'm thinking real hard.
The last time this happened,
Janet said,
       "Geeish. You can count on old Retard to goof it up."

The teacher said, "Can anyone help Patrick?"
Janet said, "Me! Me!"
When she finished,
the teacher said, "That's VERY good, Janet."

The one really wonderful thing is my lamb, Fluffy.
Fluffy is my very own lamb. He's MINE!
His mother wouldn't feed him when he was born
and Dad said I could have him if I took care of him.
I've been giving him his bottle,
and brushing him and holding him . . .
  but mostly I *talk* to Fluffy.

I tell him everything that happens at school.
He never laughs at me.
He's the ONLY ONE
who knows everything about me.

I told Fluffy about the time I heard
Mom and Dad talking.
Mom said, "Well, we produced *one* bright son.
I wonder what we did wrong with Patrick?"

And Dad said, "Patrick may not go to college . . ."
"Be serious," Mom said, "at this rate
he may not make it past grade school."

"Something is wrong with him.
We just need to face up to the fact
that he's retarded."

And, Fluffy,
remember when
I knocked over the milk
at supper
and Dad
banged his fist
on the table
and said,

"Don't you get tired
of being stupid?
THINK, Son, THINK!"

One night when Patrick was
in the barn alone with Fluffy,
the lamb snuggled up close
and in a gentle, soft voice
began to talk:

"Patrick,
some of how
you see yourself
depends on
how you think
your parents see you.

"If enough people
tell you you're inferior,
you start believing them."

Fluffy's voice was low and sometimes it cracked
because he hadn't talked much before.
But he continued,

"MOST people
feel badly about themselves
in some way.
Sometimes people
make fun of you
because they
don't feel good about themselves.
They are handicapped
by their attitudes."

Fluffy had never talked so much
in his whole life.

*"Patrick", he said, "sometimes
I don't know the answer.
Sometimes YOU don't.
Nobody knows ALL the
right answers.*

*"Your specialness
is not based on
how you look,
or how smart
you are."*

And Patrick said,

"Fluffy, I know you love me.
You're my lamb. You HAVE to.
But, I want somebody to be PROUD of me."

And Fluffy said,

*"Maybe feeling dumb
is an excuse not to try.
You find it hard to read. I know that.
We all find SOME THINGS hard — very hard.
You have to work 3 times harder
than the others, don't you?"*

*"I know you can do it if you try.
You can give up.
Or you can work like crazy."*

Patrick hung his head.
He knew it was the truth.
My Dad said I am lazy
and don't try hard enough.

"No," I told him, "I'm
just dumb.
I even look dumb
in the mirror."

But Fluffy interrupted,

*"But you can learn
to be good at something.
It won't just happen.
You must
work at it."*

Patrick had so much to think about.
He leaned on the fence and watched Fluffy with his
lamb friends.
He thought, this fence protects the sheep.
It keeps them from wandering away.
We use the fence because we love our sheep.

Maybe Fluffy told me to work hard because
he wanted to protect me from feeling
even worse about myself.
It was an interesting thought.

But *how*, Fluff,
How do I *do* it?

Just then Fluffy saw Patrick
and ran lickety-split over to the fence
prancing and wiggling his tail.
Patrick called out,

"What can I do to change, Fluffy?"

And Fluffy said,

*"Think of as many ways to solve
the problems at school as you can,
then to start with,
pick ONE."*

And Fluffy was gone again.

Okay, Fluff,
maybe if I practiced reading to you every
night in the barn that would help.

And maybe Grandpa would help me
with my spelling words.

"Way to go, Patrick!
WAY TO GO!"

"It's your attitude
that will make or break you,
not how smart or
good looking you are!"

That night after dinner,
Patrick sat on the porch with Grandpa
and they worked on the spelling words.
When they were done he said,

"There's something else, Poppy.
The kids are mean to me at school . . .
especially Jamie.
Jamie is the meanest kid who ever lived."

"You can choose to ignore Jamie, if you will.
When he teases you, just pretend to
hop on your horse and gallop away.
It won't be any fun for Jamie
if you won't listen to him."

"JAMIE IS NOT THE BOSS OF HOW YOU FEEL."

"Patrick,
when you play by yourself at school
you may feel safe,
but you also shut out loving, close friendships.
You need a friend."

"I have Fluffy, Grandpa."

"Yes, but you need a 'people friend'."

"I can teach you
how to make a friend,
Patrick."

Patrick wanted to tell Fluffy
about all of this.
When he reached the barn,
Fluffy snuggled up
with his cold nose at Patrick's neck.

Fluffy listened and listened.
Finally he said,

"Sometimes a sheep gets stuck on his back
and can't get up without help.
You're stuck, Patrick, but you can change.
You just need some help."

"Some of these hard experiences
help make you stronger.
You'll see."

"Patrick,
  Do you love me because I'm smart?"
And Patrick said,
  "No."
  "Do you love me because I'm good?"
And Patrick chuckled and said,
  "No."
  "Then, do you love me
    because I'm beautiful?"
Patrick looked at
his dirty fleece and said,
  "No."

  "Well, then, why DO
    you love me, Patrick?"
Patrick started to cry
and said, "I love you
because you're mine."

And with that, Fluffy said,
  "Patrick, look at me.
    Look me right in the eye:

    "Patrick Edward Parker,
      I LOVE YOU."

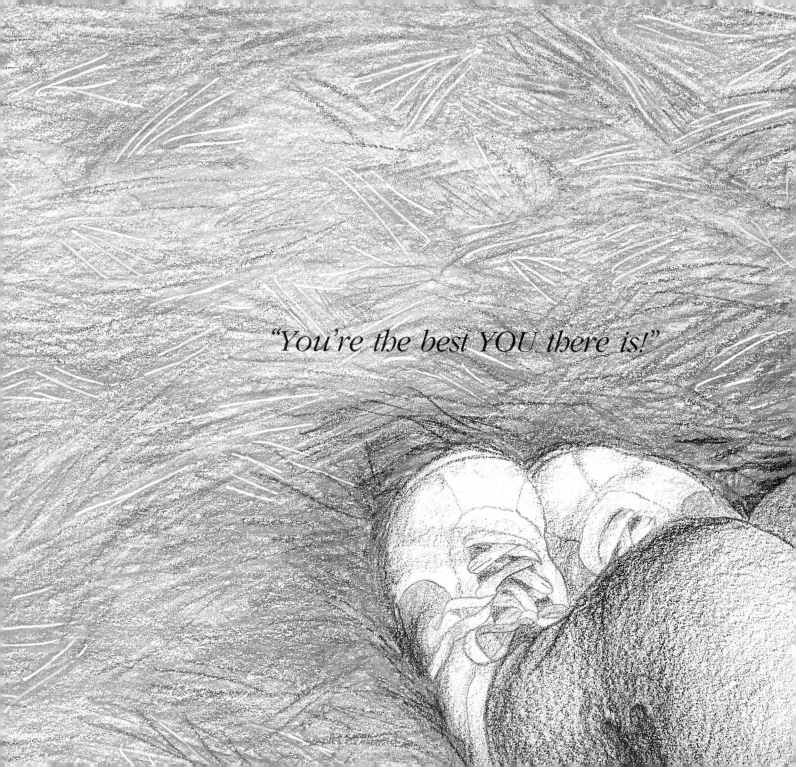

"You're the best YOU there is!"

Dear Friend,

Self-hatred may be deeply ingrained in a child by the time he reaches school age. Perhaps you know a child who does not feel good about himself. Here are some suggestions that may help:

1. *One good friend can offset many painful experiences. Friends provide the support and love a child must have to feel acceptable.*

2. *Admire a child's accomplishments and encourage the child's pride in his own work.*

3. *Help a child learn new ways of dealing with problems by anticipating what a situation may be like and how he might respond.*

4. *Emotionally healthy children have lasting, loving relationships with at least one adult during childhood.*

5. *A child needs to count on an adult to be there for him, to meet his physical needs, to protect him, and provide rules and structure.*

6. *Teach a child to be assertive in getting his needs met and to ask for help. Say, "Come tell me and I'll help you" when a child is taunted by peers.*